W9-AQW-148

KATIE WOO

and PEDRO

Mysteries

The Mystery of the Missing Mummy

by Fran Manushkin

illustrated by Tammie Lyon

PICTURE WINDOW BOOKS
a capstone imprint

Published by Picture Window Books, an imprint of Capstone
1710 Roe Crest Drive, North Mankato, Minnesota 56003
capstonepub.com

Text copyright © 2023 by Fran Manushkin
Illustrations copyright © 2023 by Capstone

Library of Congress Cataloging-in-Publication Data is available
on the Library of Congress website.

ISBN: 9781666335859 (hardcover)
ISBN: 9781666335804 (paperback)
ISBN: 9781666335811 (ebook PDF)

Summary: After learning about mummies, Katie Woo decides to make one of
her own. She leaves it in the sun to dry, and when she and Pedro go to check
on the mummy, it's missing! Can Katie and Pedro collect clues that lead
them to the missing mummy?

Design Elements by Shutterstock: Darcraft, Magnia
Designed by Dina Her

Printed and bound in the USA. PO4882

Table of Contents

Chapter 1

Mummies Are Cool!

Katie was reading about

mummies in school.

"Wow!" she said. "I found

a lady mummy. Her name

was Hatshepsut."

"That's a good find,"
said Miss Winkle. "She was a
ruler in Egypt. It took many
years to find and dig out her
mummy."

Katie looked at lots of pictures of mummies. She told Pedro, "Mummies are spooky, but kind of cool."

After school, Katie walked

home with Pedro and Davy,

the new boy next door.

Davy told Katie, "My dad put

up a tent. Come and see it!"

"I can't," said Katie. "I'm going to make a mummy!"

"Right now?" asked Davy.

"Yes!" said Katie. "I'm in a hurry to have my own mummy."

Katie told Pedro, "Come inside with me. My dad is baking cookies. When they are done, you can help us eat them."

"Thanks!" said Pedro. "I'm a great helper."

Katie began making her mummy. She made the case out of cardboard. Then she painted it blue and gold and pink. She used a lot of paint!

Katie told Pedro, "Mummies need something dead inside. I'll use Koko's bone. It's a perfect shape for a mummy."

"For sure," said Pedro. "Plus, it's old and smelly."

Chapter 2

Mummy Gone Missing

"The paint needs time to dry," said Katie. "Let's leave the mummy outside in the sunshine."

Katie and Pedro went

inside to eat cookies. When

they came back outside,

Katie got a big surprise.

Her mummy was gone!

Katie saw her dog digging!

She said, "Maybe Koko is trying to bury her bone that is in my mummy!"

But no! Koko was digging out her old tennis ball.

"Let's hurry around the
block," said Pedro. "We will
find the mummy thief! That
boy is holding something
colorful. Maybe it's your
mummy!"

"Stop!" Pedro yelled. The boy stopped.

"Oops!" said Katie. "We thought you had my mummy. But it's a guitar."

"Right!" The boy smiled. "I'll play a tune for you."

"Great!" said Katie. "Later!"

Pedro and Katie began

running again.

"Look!" Pedro pointed.

"I see pink drops on the

sidewalk. Your mummy has

pink paint, and it was not

dry! Let's follow these drips!"

The drips went around

the corner. Katie and

Pedro followed them. They

followed them to a boy

eating pink ice cream.

"Phooey!" said Katie.

"Bad clue."

Chapter 3
Mystery Solved

"Let's go home," said Katie. "We will never find my mummy."

They walked past a toy store filled with fancy mummies.

"They look terrific," said Katie. "But I love my mummy best."

Katie and Pedro walked into her yard. Davy, the boy next door, was playing in his yard.

"Uh, hi," said Davy. His face was red.

"What's wrong?" asked

Katie.

"Um, nothing," said Davy.

"Hey!" said Pedro. "Your

hands are very colorful."

"You caught me!" said Davy. "I took Katie's mummy. I took it to surprise you."

"Oh?" asked Katie. "What's the surprise?"

"I was pretending my new tent is a pyramid," said Davy. "A pyramid needs a mummy inside. I wanted to surprise you with a mummy party."

"What's that?" asked Katie.

Davy smiled. "It's when we go inside my tent and eat your dad's cookies. I smelled them baking."

"Cool idea!" said Katie.

It was a tasty party!

About the Author

Fran Manushkin is the author of Katie Woo, the highly acclaimed fan-favorite early-reader series, as well as the popular Pedro series. Her other books include *Happy in Our Skin*, *Plenty of Hugs!*, *Baby, Come Out!*, and the best-selling board books *Big Girl Panties* and *Big Boy Underpants*. There is a real Katie Woo: Fran's great-niece, but she doesn't get into as much trouble as the Katie in the books. Fran lives in New York City, three blocks from Central Park, where she can often be found bird-watching and daydreaming. She writes at her dining room table, without the help of her naughty cats, Goldy and Chaim.

About the Illustrator

Tammie Lyon, the illustrator of the Katie Woo and Pedro series, says that these characters are two of her favorites. Tammie has illustrated work for Disney, Scholastic, Simon and Schuster, Penguin, HarperCollins, and Amazon Publishing, to name a few. She is also an author/illustrator of her own stories. Her first picture book, *Olive and Snowflake*, was released to starred reviews from *Kirkus* and *School Library Journal*. Tammie lives in Cincinnati, Ohio, with her husband, Lee, and two dogs, Amos and Artie. She spends her days working in her home studio in the woods, surrounded by wildlife and, of course, two mostly-always-sleeping dogs.

Glossary

clue (KLOO)—something that helps someone find something or solve a mystery

Egypt (EE-jipt)—a country in Africa

Hatshepsut (hat-SHEP-soot)—ruler of Egypt from 1479–1458 BCE

mummy (MUH-mee)—a body that has been preserved with special salts and cloth

pyramid (PIHR-uh-mid)—a large, ancient Egyptian stone structure used as a tomb for a ruler. The pyramid shape has a square base and triangular sides that meet in a point at the top.

ruler (ROO-ler)—a person who rules or governs

All About Mysteries

A mystery is a story where the main characters must figure out a puzzle or solve a crime. Let's think about *The Mystery of the Missing Mummy*.

Plot

In a mystery, the plot focuses on solving a problem. What is the problem in this story?

Clues

To solve a mystery, readers should look for clues. What are some of the clues in this mystery?

Red Herrings

Red herrings are bad clues. They do not help solve the mystery. Sometimes they even make the mystery harder to solve. What clues in this story were red herrings?

Thinking About the Story

1. Katie learned about mummies at the start of this story. Take some time to read about mummies from a book or on the internet. Then list five facts about mummies.

2. At the start of chapter 3, how did Katie feel? How do you know?

3. Were you surprised when you learned who took the mummy? Why or why not?

4. Have you ever had a treasured item go missing? Did you find it again? Write about what happened.

A Mummy for You

Katie made a mummy out of her dog's bone. You can make a mummy of your own using an old doll or figurine. This project will change how your toy looks and feels, so be sure to pick a toy that you no longer want to play with!

Make a Mummy

What you need:

- old 11.5-inch doll or a similarly sized action figure

- masking tape

- paint

- paint brushes

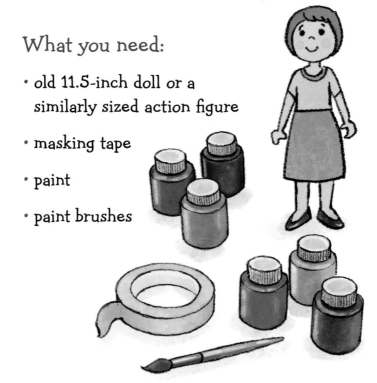

What you do:

1. Wrap the doll in masking tape so that the doll is completely covered. You can add bulk to the head area by scrunching up tape and sticking it to the neck. Then wrap more tape around that area.

2. Using paint, add the details of an ancient Egyptian sarcophagus. (That's the case that holds a mummy.) You can paint a face on the head area and add lines, shapes, and other details all over the mummy. Not sure what to paint? Look up *sarcophagus* on the internet to get some ideas!

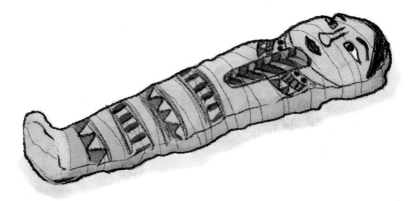

Solve more mysteries with Katie and Pedro!

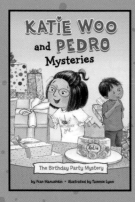

KATIE WOO and PEDRO Mysteries

The Birthday Party Mystery

by Fran Manushkin • illustrated by Tammie Lyon

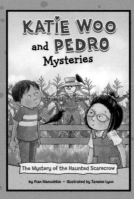

KATIE WOO and PEDRO Mysteries

The Mystery of the Haunted Scarecrow

by Fran Manushkin • illustrated by Tammie Lyon

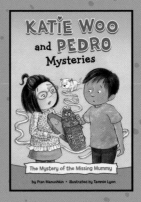

KATIE WOO and PEDRO Mysteries

The Mystery of the Missing Mummy

by Fran Manushkin • illustrated by Tammie Lyon

KATIE WOO and PEDRO Mysteries

The Mystery of the Snow Puppy

by Fran Manushkin • illustrated by Tammie Lyon

KATIE WOO and PEDRO Mysteries

The Mystery of the Stinky, Spooky Night

by Fran Manushkin • illustrated by Tammie Lyon

KATIE WOO and PEDRO Mysteries

The Peanut Butter and Jelly Mystery

by Fran Manushkin • illustrated by Tammie Lyon

KATIE WOO and PEDRO Mysteries

The Rainbow Mystery

by Fran Manushkin • illustrated by Tammie Lyon

KATIE WOO and PEDRO Mysteries

The Super-Duper Supermoon Mystery

by Fran Manushkin • illustrated by Tammie Lyon